To Harrison

Great life and
great mo...

Best wishes!

Alan McMurdo

October 2018

D1303903

To Harrison - the boy we love to watch
grow up running around church and playing on
instagram. You are blessed with a wonderful
family here on earth and in heaven! The Hanks

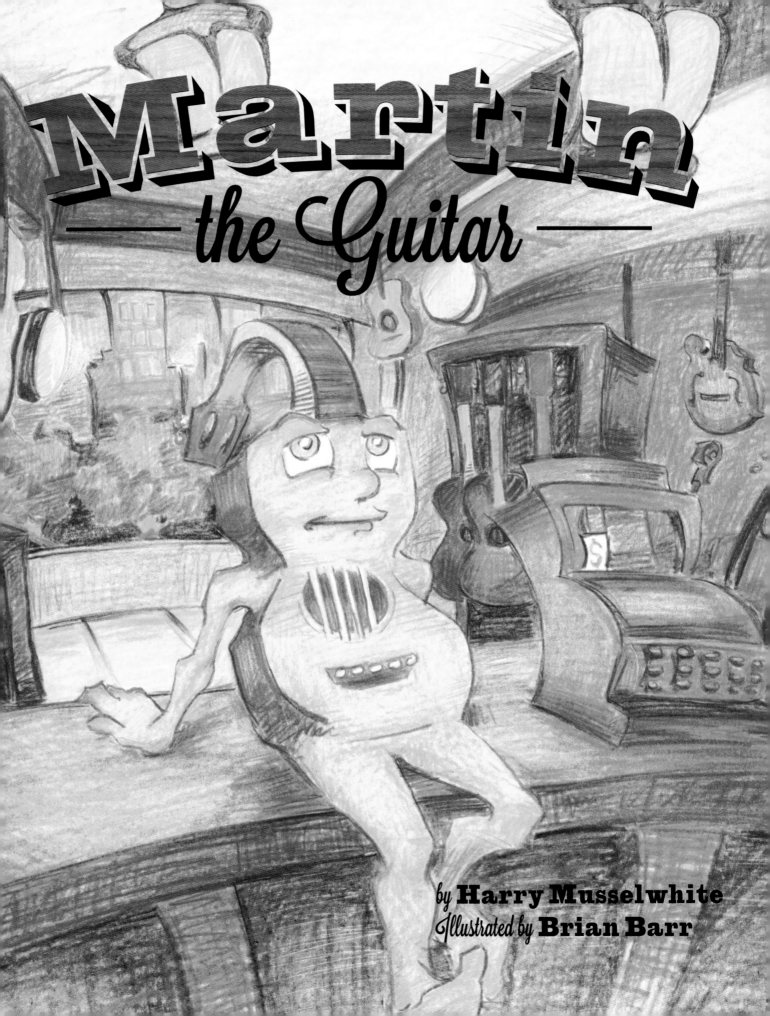

Martin
the Guitar

by **Harry Musselwhite**
Illustrated by **Brian Barr**

From Harry:
This book goes out to Laura, Dory, and Austin, and especially to Mom and Dad, who so wonderfully gave me my first guitar! Thanks!

From Brian:
I would like to lovingly dedicate this book to Mom, Dad, Carrie and Bre!

CD Credits

Mr. Beninato's Music Store *Written by Harry Musselwhite. Guitars, Mandolin, Bass: Harry Musselwhite.*
Martin's Dream *Written by Harry Musselwhite. Guitars: Harry Musselwhite.*
Gibson's Stroll *Written by Harry Musselwhite. Guitar: Harry Musselwhite, Banjo: Wesley Scheidt.*
Big D's Song *Written by Harry Musselwhite. Guitars: Harry Musselwhite.*
Martin and Strada's Song *Written by Harry Musselwhite. Guitar, Synth: Harry Musselwhite.*
Martin's Song *Written by Harry Musselwhite. Guitar: Harry Musselwhite.*

Recorded at Berry College Music Studios.
Produced and Engineered by Elizabeth Robbins.
Mastered by Elizabeth Robbins and Stan Pethel.
Special Thanks to Stan Pethel and the Berry College Dept. of Fine Arts.
Harry Musselwhite played the Martin D-28, J-40 and OM-21 guitars.

Words and Story © 2012 by Harry Musselwhite

Illustrations © 2012 by Brian Barr

Art direction and design by Monica Sheppard, 7 Visuals

Much thanks to Mr. Dick Boak, of C.F. Martin & Company for his valuable assistance in the development of this book.

ISBN 978-1-57424-280-5

Copyright © 2011 CENTERSTREAM Publishing, LLC
P.O. Box 17878 - Anaheim Hills, CA 92817

www.centerstream-usa.com

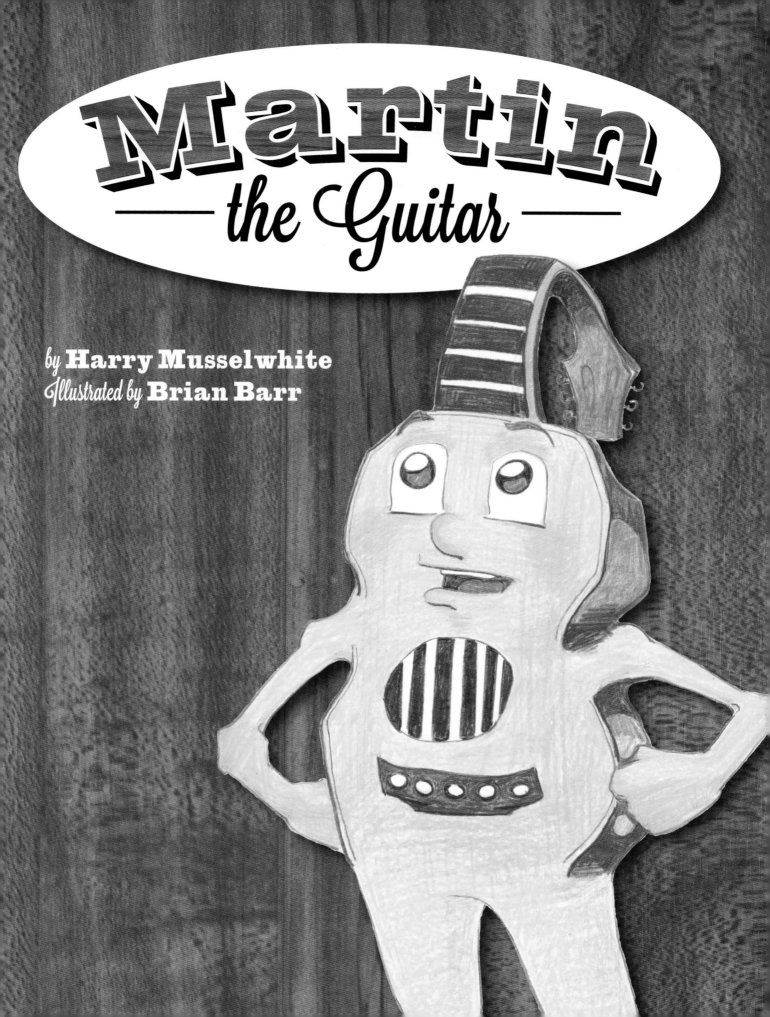

Martin
the Guitar

by **Harry Musselwhite**
Illustrated by **Brian Barr**

Martin the Guitar lived in the most famous music store in New York City. Martin stood proudly at the front of a long line of beautiful guitars of all shapes and sizes. Martin's special soft sweet tone, shiny gold keys, and polished wood made him a favorite of the owner, Mr. Carlo Beninato.

Mr. Beninato's father, Luigi, came from Italy many years ago on a steamship and built the music store on a beautiful tree-lined street near the Hudson River. People who walked in front of the shop always stopped and admired the beautiful musical instruments in the store window. World-famous musicians came to Beninato's Music Shop to try out the marvelous instruments. The musicians filled the store with sweet musical sounds.

At the back of the store stood a large portrait of Carlo's father, Luigi Beninato. Carlo was proud of his father's portrait and every day he would polish the frame before opening the front door for business. In a glass case in front of the portrait sat another important resident of Beninato's Music Shop: Strada the Violin.

Strada was one of the most famous violins in the whole world, and in the old days Luigi had played Strada in orchestras in the greatest cities of Europe. Now Strada never leaves her case and always sleeps on a velvet rug right in front of Luigi's portrait.

Often a member of one of New York's finest orchestras would march in humming a tune from a famous symphony. Musicians would often beg Carlo to let them play Strada, but he would always politely refuse and look up at his father's portrait and give him a wink.

The apple of Carlo's eye was Martin the Guitar. When Martin first came to the shop, Carlo placed a card right in front of Martin. The card read: "Instrument of the Month".

Scruffy folk musicians would enter the shop and immediately pick up Martin and play a chord. Carlo would stand nearby and beam as the soft sounds floated from Martin's strings. But when the folk musicians played Martin's big brothers, the Dreadnoughts, they always purchased them instead.

The Dreadnoughts made a loud sound, and the folk musicians felt they needed louder instruments. Carlo would make the sale and sigh as the customers exited.

"Some day, my little friend, you will find the perfect owner," whispered Carlo.

Every day Martin would make his best sounds, but he never found an owner. Carlo loved the music Martin made, but he soon took down the "Instrument of the Month" sign and moved Martin down the row behind the Dreadnoughts, or Big D's, as they were called in the shop.

Martin became very sad, and soon his strings didn't shimmer as they used to, and sometimes his soft tone was so soft one could hardly hear it.

Martin wanted to be placed in the spot of honor as instrument of the month in front of all the Big D's. He may have been one of the smallest guitars in the shop, but nobody seemed to want him. Once a day Mr. Beninato would come by and pat Martin on the shoulder. Mr. Beninato knew that Martin was a wonderful instrument, but he wondered if Martin would ever find a home. This made Mr. Beninato very sad.

All day long, Mr. Beninato scurried from one customer to another. He made small repairs on some instruments, selected sets of strings for others, and rang up sales on his old antique brass cash register.

By the end of the day, Mr. Beninato was quite tired. He went to the front door, and just before he turned out the lights, he bid his instruments good evening.

"Good night all you noble instruments," he said.

"Good night, Martin — a special sweet rest to you," he said.

And with a twinkle in his eye, Mr. Beninato looked up at his father's portrait.

"Good night, Papa," he said.

Mr. Beninato always felt he could hear his father's voice call out softly, "and good night to you, dear son."

Mr. Beninato turned out the lights, took one last look around, locked the door, and set off down the street for his evening meal.

The magic
was about
to begin...

As if rousing from a deep sleep, all the instruments in the shop began to yawn and stretch. A sweet note from a violin sounded and a deep bass note from a guitar answered. From the floor of the store came the "plink, plank" of the banjo string.

At the end of the long row of very expensive guitars yawned Martin the Guitar. Suddenly a big voice echoed throughout the store.

"Tonight I will begin our evening concert," came the booming voice of Big D.

Big D was the largest guitar in the shop, and he had the place of honor at the front of the guitar row. Big D had golden tuners, pearl highlights, and his body was made of rare wood from across the sea.

A shimmering chord sang out from Big D's strings and the entire shop grew quiet. Big D's voice rang out throughout the store, and all the other instruments listened with admiration and respect.

The music from Big D's body was pure rock and roll. All the other instruments moved in time to the driving rhythm. Every instrument in the store swayed to the melody and tapped in time to the funky beat. At the end of Big D's solo, all the instruments cheered.

"Thank you one and all," said Big D with his basso profondo voice.

Big D looked around the shop and the instruments turned their faces toward him with great expectation. It was a great honor to be chosen to follow the great D's nightly solo.

Big D didn't choose the next instrument that night. He asked a question.

"Who would like to perform next?"

The room became as quiet as a church. A few instruments coughed nervously.

Suddenly from the back of the room a sweet small voice called.

"I, I, uh, I'd like to play!," said Martin the Guitar.

All the faces turned to the back of the shop.

"Who said that?" boomed Big D.

"I did!" answered Martin.

"It's the kid," cackled Loar the Mandolin. Loar was one of the most expensive instruments in the shop, and he often shared jokes with Big D about the other instruments.

The banjos on the floor of the shop all joined in with laughter. Loar joined in their laughter and looked at Big D for approval.

"Silence!" shouted Big D.

The laughter stopped at once. No one liked to anger the Big D.

"Well, little Martin," said Big D, "do you think you've got what it takes to play for this important crowd?"

All the other instruments started murmuring to each other, doubting Martin's ability.

Suddenly a cultured and elegant voice pierced the chatter.

"I think you should give him a chance, Mr. Dreadnought," announced Strada the Violin.

The instruments in Mr. Beninato's music shop had never heard the voice of one the most famous violins in the world. Big D and all the instruments froze at the sound of Strada's silky voice.

Like a noble queen, Strada walked to the front of the store and stood right in front of Big D. All the other guitars took a step back, but Big D stood his ground.

"Well, Mr. Dreadnought, what do you think?" asked Strada.

"Uh, ah, uh...."stammered Big D.

"Speak up, guitar!" demanded Strada. "Or do you need a mandolin to do the talking for you?"

Strada turned her gaze to Loar the Mandolin, who shrunk back immediately.

Members of the violin family began to speak up in support of Strada.

"Yeah, let him play!" said one cello.

"He has a right just like anybody else," said another cello.

A big, but very shy, string bass stood above the cellos and called, "Yeah, we're tired of you always being the big boss, Mr. D!"

Big D gave the tall string bass a very mean look, and the instrument shrunk back to his corner of the shop.

Strada turned to Big D.

"Well?"

"Oh, alright!" said Big D angrily, and he stomped off.

Strada turned to Martin the Guitar, who was beginning to get nervous about his bold move.

"Okay, young man," she cooed, "make that sweet music that you love to make."

Martin turned around and saw all the instruments looking at him. The banjos were making terrible faces, but the violins smiled from bridge to neck.

Martin took a deep breath, and a waterfall of notes fell from his six strings. Each cascade of notes, soft and sweet, called up more and more beautiful sounds until the shop was filled with a river of string sound the likes of which had never been heard in Beninato's Music Shop!

Now being the smallest guitar in the shop didn't matter anymore. What mattered was the music spilling out of Martin the Guitar.

As the melody from Martin's body began to swell, even Strada came under the small guitar's spell. All of a sudden, Strada's magnificent voice soared over Martin's notes and the two played a duet that held all the instruments in awe.

Higher and higher Strada sang, and without fear, Martin the Guitar played as she flew. Strada's eyes closed as she played notes she had not thought about in years. At the back of the shop, her brother and sister violins wiped tears of joy from their eyes. Even the banjos, who had never heard such music, were overcome with musical delight.

The duet slowly came to an end, and Strada stopped playing in order to listen to Martin the Guitar's last few chords. At last, only one note rang out from the guitar's lowest string. Martin held his breath. The store was silent.

Then every instrument erupted in shouts and cheers.

"Hooray for Martin!" rang the cellos.

"Three cheers for Martin the Guitar!" yelled the shy string bass. Big D walked up to Martin and the room grew quiet.

Big D slapped Martin on the back and crowed, "Instrument of the Month!"

Everyone took up Big D's cheer, and "Instrument of the Month" rang out through the store.

With a sigh and a smile, Strada turned and walked back to her glass case. All the instruments quickly formed a double line and bowed as she majestically marched back to her case. Just before she got into the glass case, she looked up at Luigi's smiling face and blew a sweet kiss at the portrait.

Martin raced back and reached her just before she lay down.

"Oh Strada, how can I ever thank you?"

"Thank me? For what, young guitar?" said Strada.

"You stood up for me and gave me the courage to do my best, " said Martin. "I thought I would never find a home, but now I know that some day soon, I will be taken from this shop by one of the best musicians around. I just know it!"

"Young Martin, you had it in you all the time. You just needed to believe in yourself."

"Believe in myself, that's it!" said Martin.

The next morning the streets of New York City were beautiful. The sun was shining and every tree on the avenue was fresh with new green leaves. It seemed all the world was in bloom as Mr. Beninato walked to his store. The beautiful day cheered Mr. Beninato. Mr. Beninato was so happy that he even whistled a tune by Mozart as he walked along.

Mr. Beninato reached his store, and as he bent down to pick up the morning paper, he noticed a note attached to his front door. He reached down and took the letter from the door.

"Dear Mr. Beninato," the letter read, "please don't sell the little shiny guitar you call Martin. I want to buy it and give it as a birthday present for my brother who is a folk singer in Georgia."

Mr. Beninato grinned from ear to ear as he unlocked the door to his shop. As he entered, he flipped on the light switch and the store burst into light.

"What?" exclaimed Mr. Beninato.

Standing at the front of the guitar row and leading a proud line of famous dreadnoughts was none other than Martin the Guitar. The sign at Martin's feet read: "Instrument of the Month".